Would you rather...

JOHN BURNINGHAM

THOMAS Y. CROWELL
New York

Other books by John Burningham

MR. GUMPY'S MOTOR CAR
COME AWAY FROM THE WATER, SHIRLEY
TIME TO GET OUT OF THE BATH, SHIRLEY

Little Books

THE BABY
THE BLANKET
THE CUPBOARD
THE DOG
THE FRIEND
THE RABBIT
THE SCHOOL
THE SNOW

Library of Congress Cataloging in Publication Data

Burningham, John
   Would you rather . . .

   SUMMARY: Presents choices for the reader such as living
with a gerbil in a cage or with a rabbit in a hutch and being
chased by a crab, by a bull, by a lion, or by wolves.
   I. Title.
PZ7. B936Wo   [E]   78–7088
ISBN 0–690–03917–4
ISBN 0–690–03918–2 (lib. bdg.)

Printed in Great Britain

Would you rather . . .

Your house was surrounded by

water

snow

or jungle

Would you rather . . .

an elephant drank your bath water

an eagle
stole your dinner

a pig tried on your clothes

or a hippo slept in your bed

Would you rather be . . .

covered in jam

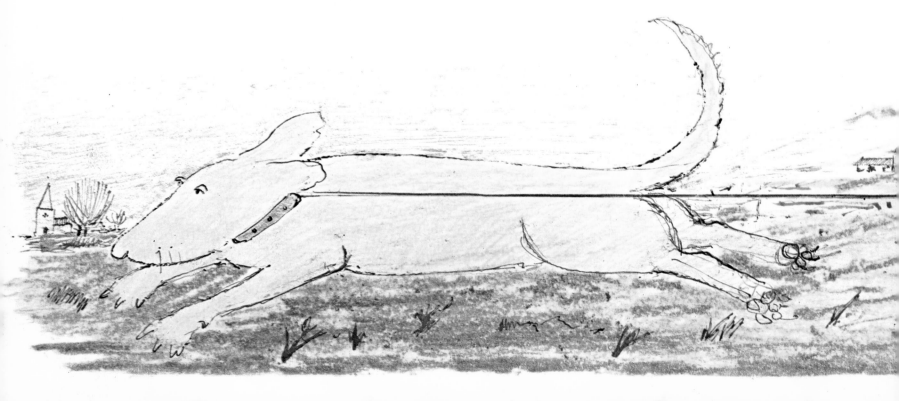

or soaked
with water

or pulled through the mud by a dog

Would you rather have . . .

supper in a castle   breakfast in a balloon

or tea on the river

Would you rather be made to eat . . .

spider stew

slug dumplings

mashed worms

or
drink
snail
squash

Would you rather . . .

jump in the brambles for 25¢

swallow a dead frog for 50¢

stay all night in a creepy house for $1.00

Would you rather . . .

be crushed by a snake

swallowed by a fish

eaten by a crocodile

or sat on by a rhinoceros

Would it be worse . . .

if your dad danced at school

or your mom made a fuss in a cafe

Would you rather . . .

clash the cymbals

bang the drum

or blow the trumpet

Would you rather . . .

know a monkey
you could tickle

a bear
you could read to

a cat
you could box with

a dog
you could skate with

a pig you could ride

or a goat you could dance with

Would you rather be chased by . . .

a crab

or a bull

or a lion

or by wolves

Or would you like to ride a bull
into a supermarket

Would you rather be lost . . .

in a fog

or at sea

in a desert

in a forest

or in a crowd

Would you rather help . . .

a fairy turn a
frog into a prince

gnomes look for treasu

an imp be naughty

a witch make a stew

or Santa Claus deliver presents

Would you rather live with . . .

a gerbil in a cage

a fish in a bowl

a parrot on a perch

a rabbit in a hutch

chickens in a coop

or a dog in a kennel

Or perhaps you would rather
just go to sleep in your own bed